For Esther, Rosen

Red's Rainbow

Published by Flower Guard Books

Southgate
Hornsea
HU18 1RE

Red's Rainbow

Andi Dawson

Red was miserable.

Everywhere he went he saw birds of different colours.

There was...
a cloud of orange,

a burst of yellow,

a canopy of green,

a sky of blue,

a sea of indigo

and a flash of violet.

Red thought he didn't belong with any of them.

Then the grey clouds filled the sunny sky and the rain fell...

...Red found his place in the world.

He was part of the rainbow of birds.

Thank you for reading Red's Rainbow.
We hope you enjoyed it.

If you did, you might like some more
stories from Flower Guard Books.
You can find them on Amazon, Facebook
or you can loan a selection of books from
East Riding Libraries.

You can get in touch with us by emailing
flowerguardbooks@yahoo.com

Never forget to dream!

Printed in Great
Britain
by Amazon